Y0-DWN-507

Stumpy's Secret

Mandy Hager
illustrated by David Elliot

Learning Media

1.
Me and Uncle Mo

I've got this story to tell you. I guess you could say there's a message in it – not a lecture-type message like my dad's always giving me, but ... man, I don't know! ... it just kind of seems important. All I know is, my life got a whole lot better after all this happened. So I'll tell you the story, and you can figure it out for yourself, OK?

It was the first day of summer vacation. I knew I was in for a bad day as soon as I stepped in the cat's little offering on my way to the bathroom. Then, as I was hopping through the doorway to wash my foot in the bathtub, I banged my knee so hard it bled. I hate it when that happens.

To top it off, Dad had left for work already, and the only thing for breakfast was oatmeal. I hate that too.

Now that school was out, I had to go to Uncle Mo's every day. It was kind of like a vacation job, but really it was so that Uncle Mo could keep an eye on me while Dad was at work. Not that I minded that, you know? Living right next door to Uncle Mo's junkyard was the best thing about my life. (The worst thing, apart from Mom being dead, was that Dad had to work all the time and I hardly ever got to see him.) You can always find something cool in Uncle Mo's yard – something you want to take home, fix up, and turn into Something-Really-Useful-If-I-Could-Only-Figure-Out-What! That's why I have a SAVE pile where I stash anything that's any use, or that might be fixable. Not the big stuff – that's Uncle Mo's business. But if any of my fixed-up treasures get sold, the profit's all mine.

Anyway, after that stinky start to the day, I was in a real bad mood by the time I squirmed through the hole in the fence to the junkyard. My plan for the day was to fix up an old skateboard that I'd found the day before. So I was headed toward my SAVE pile, right, when a movement down by the car wrecks caught my eye. A figure, hunched and gray, vanished into the glare of the morning sun. There was something familiar about it ... but by the time I'd run over there (and believe me, my wounded knee was *not* in the mood to run), the yard was empty.

Well, not exactly empty – it is a junkyard, after all. Miles and miles of it to be exact. I'm not saying it's messy – no way. Not when you know Uncle Mo's system. Car parts, old furniture, scrap metal, broken appliances, whatever – they've all got their proper places. It's my job to check everything that comes in, and I gotta say, there's more treasure hidden in other people's trash than in all the shipwrecks in the world. No kidding! I mean, people throw things out that just need a screw here or a new part there .... And then there's old chairs – talk about buried treasure! Slide your hand down the back and the sides – deep down, where people forget to look. I've found coins, magazines, TV remotes, model cars – even the odd big note, on a real good day.

But to get back to my story – this was *not* a good day. By the time I'd run the length of that yard, I was crosser than a critter in a trap. I limped back to my stash, next to the big old pink limousine that Uncle Mo bought from some dying movie star. (My inheritance, he called it.)

I hated it when he said that. (Death talk makes me freak, what with Mom and all.)

It was then that I noticed that my sign, "You Touch – You Suffer," was swinging madly in the breeze. Only there wasn't any breeze. And my carefully stashed skateboard, a wall fan, and a birdcage were all gone.

2.
Searching
for Stumpy

was furious. To me, that stuff's not junk, it's freedom. It's my only source of money, see. No money means no treats – if you can call new shoes a treat. That's what I was saving for. Sure, Dad had just got me this pair of shoes from the Goodwill, hardly worn – but I have to tell you, they're really gross. There's no way I'm wearing them to school. The kids already think I'm weird, just because my dad won't let me roam the streets at night like the rest of them. (Not that I *want* to – streets are dangerous. People die roaming the streets.) Besides, that junk also pays for me to get into the movies and stuff like that.

Yep, I was fuming, all right. It didn't make sense. No one around here would rip off Uncle Mo like that – he's real popular in this neighborhood.

He was in the Marines before he bought this yard, and the way he talks, you'd think he'd circled the world about fifty times. He knows stuff you'd never even dream about. People visit the yard just to hear his stories. My dad reckons that the only thing well traveled about his brother is his mouth, but maybe he's just jealous of Uncle Mo's popularity. Dad's more the serious type. I guess he doesn't have a whole lot to laugh about.

Then it hit me. That figure I'd spotted – it *had* to be that old coot Stumpy. Always snooping around the yard, running his filthy old hands over everything … he'd be mean enough to swipe my stash.

Stumpy wasn't his real name, of course. I always thought of him that way because he had most of one finger missing. The creepy part was, he could still move the stump of it – like those pathetic dogs that have their tails cut off, and all they can wag is that poor little stub. Uncle Mo didn't seem to mind old Stumpy, even stopped to chat if he noticed him in the yard. But he gave me the creeps, always trying to ruffle my hair or talk about my mom. He had to be my thief, for sure.

I remembered he always carried a grubby old sack. I had to get that sack and catch the old devil out. I figured he couldn't be too far away. He'd be heading back to his shop on Port Street. I used to visit that old dive when I was a kid. Truth is, it was his shop that gave me the idea of starting my own. Uncle Mo reckons it was the most successful repair shop for miles around, once upon a time. Now it's full to bursting with so much weird old stuff, you can't even see what's there.

I scrambled over the fence by the tire mountain, into the Maxwells' yard. I didn't like to do that, but it saved precious minutes. Mungo, their scabby greyhound, looked up from his favorite hole under the house and woofed. That made me run even faster. It wasn't that I was scared of Mungo – he wouldn't hurt a fly. But I'd heard that Mrs. Maxwell's no-good stepson, Crazy Ken, had broken out of jail again. It wasn't likely he'd be hiding out there, but if he was, I didn't want Mungo telling him I was snooping around.

Luckily, the place seemed empty. I sneaked around the side of the house and out to the street. I half expected to find old Stumpy right there, but the crafty old guy was faster than I thought. I kept running, sure I'd catch him by the shopping center.

His store was wedged between a Laundromat and a Chinese takeout. You could just read the faded sign above the door: "Carducci Collectables and Curios." Carducci – that was Stumpy's real name. Italian, I guess. He has a kind of singa-songa way of talking, like the bad guys in those old gangster movies.

I peered through the dusty window, but there was so much junk piled inside, I couldn't see a thing. I thought maybe I'd take a look out the back, but just as I squeezed myself down the dark gap between the buildings, a hand clamped down hard on my shoulder.

3.
To Catch
a Thief

I jumped so bad my head crashed into the rough brick wall.

"What're you doing here, Joe?" It was Uncle Mo.

"Old Stumpy," I complained. "He stole my stash."
The words came out whiny, and I could see Uncle
Mo frown under his hairy-caterpillar eyebrows.

"What? You *think* he stole it, or you *saw*
him?" Uncle Mo gripped my arm and steered
me toward home. "Think hard, Joe. You oughta
know by now there's an awful big difference
between the two." He wasn't often serious
like this, but when he was, he sounded just
like Dad.

"Who else could it be?" I mumbled. "He's
always poking around, and that sack of his is
full of *something*." I wished Uncle Mo would
slow down. His big hand was hurting my arm,
and my knee was bleeding again.

Uncle Mo shook his head. "Old Edmondo was
quite a guy in his day, you know. He had this
wife who was so-o-o beautiful she'd break your
heart. Pride used to shine out of that guy's face
like a beacon, Joe." He relaxed then, his voice
dropping into storytelling mode. "You needed
something fixed, Edmondo was the Man.
Nothing was too tricky – or too much trouble."

"Shame he lost his touch then." I didn't mean it to come out quite so sarcastic, but my head had started throbbing, and all I could think about was the pain that miserable old man had caused me.

Uncle Mo didn't reply, but he folded his arms and stormed on ahead of me, so I knew he was mad. I'd have to catch Stumpy in the act. Then maybe Uncle Mo would believe me.

Uncle Mo was sore at me for the rest of the day. As soon as I'd cleaned myself up a bit, he handed me the nail-pullers and pointed toward the stack of recycled lumber. My worst job! But at least it gave me plenty of time to plan ....

I laid my best treasures out on the old table beside the pink limo and set The Trap. First I stretched a tripwire, cut from a rusty old roll I'd saved, all around the table. Then I added the magic ingredient. Bells! Ages ago, I'd found this box full of bells that I thought were real silver, until Uncle Mo put me straight. The silver plating was curling at the edges now, but they still tinkled loud enough to do the job I had in mind.

Once the trap was set, I moved into Phase Two. Dad made this part easy. Every night after supper, he'd watch TV for about an hour, then he'd fall asleep on the couch.

As soon as I heard him start to snore, I bunched up my dirty clothes and stuffed them under my blanket to look like I was in bed. Careful not to make any noise, I opened my bedroom window and climbed out.

It was one of those nights where every sound seems twenty times louder than usual. By the time I'd crept past all the spooky shadows of the yard, I'd almost lost my nerve. I'd left a sleeping bag inside the limo, and I snuggled down inside that bag double-quick. The cracked leather of the car seat felt scratchy and cold against my face as I lay down and stared at an old framed photo of my mom that I kept in there. Then the day caught up with me, and I yawned. Maybe I'd just shut my eyes for a minute ....

4.
Dogged by Disaster

When those bells started ringing in the middle of the night, I nearly died of fright. The sleeping bag had swallowed me like a giant snake, and fear fuzzed my brain. I fought my way out of the bag and the car, with the bells going crazy. I could see a dark shape hunched over my treasure, looking like some spooky creature from the grave. But I had to catch it – if only to shut up the terrible tinkling, which echoed around the yard like Christmas gone mad.

With a screech, I threw myself at the hunched figure. My hands struck something soft and held on tight. Together, the monster and I rolled onto the ground. It turned its face toward me … and licked me on the nose. Mungo! That darned dog had set off my bells. I was so hyped up I couldn't stop laughing, especially when I realized that the poor mutt had some plastic cord caught around his skinny tail, and it was tangled in my trip wire. So every time silly old Mungo wagged his tail, the cord rattled the bells – like a doggy Quasimodo from *The Hunchback of Notre Dame*.

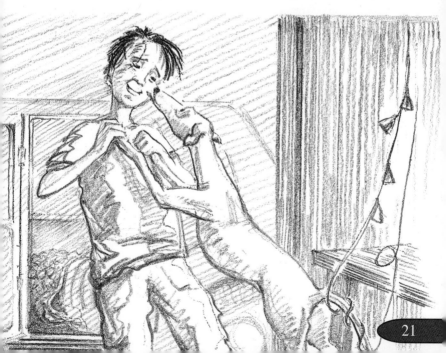

I managed to calm Mungo down and unhook him from the trap. When the last bell stopped tinkling, the night was so quiet it felt unreal. I walked the old dog through the yard and boosted him up over the fence toward his home. It must've been after four because the sky was starting to glow.

As I scooped my sleeping bag off the ground, I glanced over at my treasure table. *Funny* .... I stepped up close and checked my stuff. The old alarm clock was missing and the little gas cooker that I'd spent three weeks fiddling with to make it work. I couldn't believe it! While I'd been snoring in the limo, old Stumpy had outsmarted me again. My good mood vanished, and I stomped back home to catch a couple of hours' sleep.

You can imagine how lousy I felt when it was time to get up again. All morning, I stumbled around the yard like a zombie. I was plodding around a corner when splat! – I crashed right into Stumpy. I knocked the poor old guy off his feet, but did I care? I was so darned mad.

"Hey, watch-a yourself, boy. What's-a the rush?"

He was right there, the old thief – right there beside me, with his bulging sack full of *my* treasure. I was just about to accuse him when Uncle Mo appeared from nowhere.

"Edmondo, my friend – are you all right?" Uncle Mo hoisted Stumpy to his feet and brushed him down. "Forgive my clumsy nephew," he said, glaring at me. "He's got a bad case of overactive imagination." I swear the old trickster winked at me as Uncle Mo helped him to his office for a cup of coffee.

Nobody even cared about my missing stuff. Uncle Mo was backing old Stumpy, and Dad was too busy to notice me at all …, I tried not to think about my mom, but I couldn't help it, as I stood there like a baby in that dusty lane, big tears of frustration pricking at my eyes.

I sat down on an old filing cabinet and checked my knee. Bleeding again. But when I glanced around for something I could use to wipe it clean, what I spotted made me punch the air in triumph. There, beside the old cartwheel at the corner of the bend – Stumpy's sack. Just waiting for me.

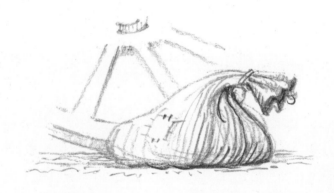

5.
Sticks and Stones and Dry Old Bones

The sack was lighter than I expected. I carried it back to the limo before I opened it up. All I could see was motley gray cotton – the stuffing that leaked from every ruined armchair in the place. I shook the sack. There was definitely something else in there. Careful not to put my hand too deep (hey, if I could set a trap, then so could he), I hooked the stuffing out then tipped the sack upside down.

Out rolled a dusty collection of … junk. Old screws, bits of wire, Popsicle sticks, smooth stones. All useless, and none of it mine. I felt kind of silly then, but I convinced myself it only proved that Stumpy was sneakier than I'd first figured.

Just as I was about to throw it all back in the sack, my hand knocked against something at the bottom of the sack. I reached right down and pulled out a small box.

It was a tobacco tin, one of those real old ones collectors go for, but it wasn't rusty like you'd expect. It was shiny and smooth, and felt almost as though it had been rubbed in someone's hands for years. Carefully, I wedged open the lid and lifted the layer of cotton.

Yuck! I dropped the tin, and the two revolting things that fell into my lap threw me into a shuddering dance of disgust. Stumpy's finger bones! They had to be. They were just the right size and shape. Why else would he store them so carefully in this tin?

After I'd recovered from the shock, I picked them up and laid them back on their bed of cotton.

Then, and don't ask me why, I slipped that tin right on into my pocket. I just had a feeling that somehow I could make use of those nasty little bones.

One of Uncle Mo's stories came to me then, about this guy who'd been shot down in the desert during the war. He'd been stumbling around, desperate for water, when he came across the remains of a human skeleton scattered in the sand. At the same moment, an enemy plane flew overhead. Without thinking, the guy picked up one of those bones and shook it at the enemy in rage. And would you believe it – the plane fell from the sky, right in front of his eyes. Spooky, huh?

Remembering that story made me feel pretty weird. I quickly crammed the sad bunch of trash back into Stumpy's sack and left it out for him to find.

I didn't waste any time getting to bed that night. Man, was I tired! But sometime in the night, I had this awful dream. It was something about a plane – it was falling, and it was on fire ….

I woke up with the stink of smoke in my nostrils. At first I thought it was the dream, but then the shouts and the alarms started, and I knew it was for real. Dad was running down the hall, and I grabbed my trousers and chased after him. I could see the flicker of flames as I scrambled through the hole into Uncle Mo's yard. Even before I reached it, I guessed where the smoke was coming from.

My limo – my fabulous pink limousine. Uncle Mo was already spraying like crazy with the big fire hose, and Dad ran up with our extinguisher to help. I grabbed the garden hose and started wetting down the stuff around the fire that might catch. By the time the fire truck arrived, poor old Uncle Mo looked beat, and as soon as the flames were out, Dad led him through the crowd of rubber-necking neighbors.

Everyone was standing around in their pajamas like a bunch of escaped hospital patients. There was Mrs. Maxwell and her horde of kids, the Stevensons, the Bernsteins, Ms. Eastermann and her crabby old father, Stumpy – *Stumpy*? What was he doing here?

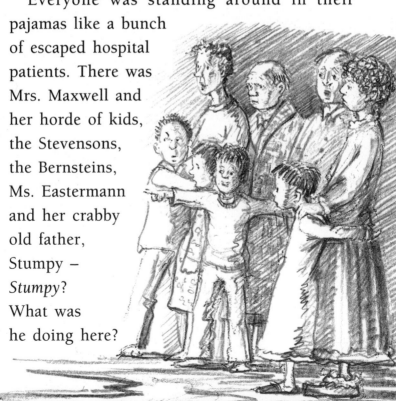

I can't explain what made me do it, but as Stumpy moved away, I dragged that old tin out of my pants pocket and held it high above my head. Maybe it was the funny look on Stumpy's face as he turned to leave, or maybe it was the weary, defeated look in Uncle Mo's eyes. Whatever it was, I was mad, real mad. I held the tin high, and just before Stumpy turned the corner, I shook those old finger bones at his thieving back with all the force that I could muster.

6.
Gigantic Guilt

We all slept late the next morning, and I didn't see Uncle Mo until nearly noon. He looked about twenty years older, and I wondered why. OK, so the limo was worth some, but it was insured, and nothing else was damaged, so what was the big deal? If anyone should have been upset, it was *me*, and I was too busy planning my revenge on Stumpy.

It was only when Uncle Mo called me into his office that I knew Something Big was up. He pointed to a chair and waited for me to sit.

"I got some bad news, Joe." Just the way he said it made my stomach flip. *Not Dad. Please, not Dad.*

"Last night, after the fire, old Edmondo ...." He paused, and I could hear my own heartbeat in the silence. "A car knocked him down. The scumbag didn't even stop."

It felt like all the air sucked out of the room. "Is he ... dead?" I had done this to him. Me. Just like that guy and the plane. *I'd killed old Stumpy.*

Uncle Mo shook his head. "No. But he's pretty bad, according to Gramps Eastermann." He was staring at me hard, like he knew it was all my fault. "It's like this, Joe, I gotta hang around here today, on account of the fire. I know you're not too hot on the old guy, but I really need to know how he's doing. They won't tell me nothin' over the phone."

I wanted to curl up into a little ball and die, like cats do when they know their time is up, but I just nodded and took the piece of paper with Stumpy's name and his ward number at the hospital.

It wasn't very far to walk, but my legs suddenly seemed filled with lead, and my brain whispered "murderer" every time I saw my reflection in a shop window. By the time I reached the hospital, I was just about gagging from nerves. The clerk at the reception desk looked me up and down.

"Are you family?" she asked.

"No." I could feel cold sweat drip down my forehead.

She frowned.
"Sorry, kid.
Family only for
Mr. Carducci today."

The hospital smells swelled around me, and my head felt woozy. I steadied myself against the wall and waited for the clerk to turn away, then I staggered up the stairs in the direction of Stumpy's ward. If Uncle Mo wanted me to check, then at least I could do that right.

The door to the ward was closed, but I pushed it open and plunged on in. I smiled at a nurse walking past as if I knew her, and tried to hide the fact that my knees had turned to jelly. Every room off the long corridor had a different little nameplate. Then I saw it. *Mr. E. Carducci*. My hand shook like crazy as I tried to wipe the sweat off my top lip.

I slipped through the partly-open door. There was Stumpy, connected to a beeping machine and wearing a mask that made a terrible sucking noise every time he breathed. I can't begin to describe the guilt that swept over me in waves – like I'd been drowned and washed up on a beach.

Before I knew it, I was running for home, and these fat, little-kid tears were pouring down my face. I couldn't stop them, and I didn't even care. I dived into bed, pulled the blankets up over my head, and rolled up tight.

That's when I really started to howl. I wasn't going to blab this, but I guess you have to know. I cried for Stumpy all right, but mainly I cried for my mom. You see, that accident, the one that killed her when I was five ... that was a hit-and-run, too. Mom was taking me to the park, and I was running ahead of her, when this car swerved up onto the sidewalk and hit her. If only she'd seen the car coming, if only she hadn't been chasing me ... maybe she'd still be alive.

I lay in that ball until there were no more tears inside me, just this big dull ache like a horse had kicked me in the guts. Finally I put my head out to check the clock on the dresser and stared straight at that old tobacco tin of Stumpy's.

Right away, I knew just what I had to do.

7.
Blind Man's Bluff

I was sure Stumpy would die and his ghost would come to claim those bones, but all of the next day, Uncle Mo kept me cleaning up the mess the fire had made. He might have been worried about Stumpy, but work still had to carry on, and that meant for me too. When I thought about it, I realized even more of my treasures were missing, but for some reason, I didn't care. Maybe I couldn't be mad with Stumpy anymore, or maybe I was just too tired and shocked to feel anything else.

So it wasn't until the following day that I managed to visit the hospital again. I stopped along the way to spend my precious savings on grapes and oranges – that's what you take to sick people, isn't it?

The tobacco tin in my pocket tapped against my leg as I climbed the stairs to Stumpy's ward. But when I poked my head into his room, I almost cried. All the machines were gone, and he lay there absolutely still. I'd arrived too late.

I remembered seeing Mom dead, and I thought I'd freak out seeing Stumpy now. But he looked kind of peaceful and a darned sight cleaner than I'd ever seen him before. I sneaked right in and placed the tin with his missing bones beside him – too late to save his life, but I figured it was the proper thing to do.

I closed my eyes. "Sorry, Stumpy," I whispered. "I'm really sorry. If I could only …."

"Only what?" Stumpy grabbed my hand as he said the words, and my heart tried to burst out through my ribs. Grapes and oranges spilled onto the floor.

"You're not … dead?" Dumb question, I know, but when a corpse speaks to you, it's hard to think straight.

Stumpy laughed wheezily and poked me with his short finger. "Takes-a more than an old car to kill-a me!" His gaze fell on the tin. "Ah. So that's-a where you got to." He picked it up and stroked the lid against his cheek.

"I … I didn't steal it," I blustered, my face hotter than a heater. "Well, OK, I did. But I came here to give it back."

Stumpy shook the tin at me. "You know what's in-a here, Joe?"

I couldn't speak. It was like those finger bones jumped down my throat and stuck there. I just nodded.

"Isabella," Stumpy crooned, and again he stroked his cheek with the tin.

"Isabella?" I squeaked out the name, totally confused.

It turned out Isabella was Stumpy's wife, who died a few years ago. But don't worry, it wasn't her bones in that crazy old man's tin. "She was bellissima, my Isabella," he whispered. "She give-a me these silly old-a bones one day for a joke-a – my lost finger, you know?" His eyes went all watery as he told me how he missed his wife more than he'd ever missed his finger. How every day he still woke up expecting to see her. How he kept those "silly old-a bones" she'd given him, but he couldn't replace the missing part of him that she took with her. And as for Stumpy's finger – would you believe, he was born that way!

I was so relieved to know that I hadn't really cursed him, I blabbed out everything. My missing stash, the fire, shaking the bones at him, everything. Stumpy didn't comment, just lay there really still with his eyes half closed. I thought he'd gone to sleep, and I was glad because I couldn't stop gabbling on, just like he'd done to me. I talked about my mom – how much I missed her, how every day I still woke up expecting to see her, how I hung onto things she'd given me ....

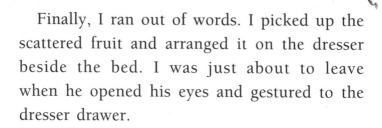

Finally, I ran out of words. I picked up the scattered fruit and arranged it on the dresser beside the bed. I was just about to leave when he opened his eyes and gestured to the dresser drawer.

There was a pair of glasses inside with the thickest lenses I'd ever seen. I gave them to Stumpy, and he put them on and motioned for me to come up close. Bit by bit, he studied my face. "Life, she's-a funny," he sighed. "I thought I never see right again. Then that stupido car hit-a me, and the doctors check-a me all over, test everything, see if they can fix-a me up." He grinned at me. "And they give-a me these."

I remembered then how he always felt his way around the yard and how he shuffled with his foot sweeping in front like a radar. Then I thought of the shop and the way he never fixed things anymore.

"Is that why you started taking my treasures – because you couldn't fix things for yourself?"

Stumpy's face grew hard. "You think I steal-a your old-a junk? Stupido boy. You gotta lot to learn."

If there had been a hole in that hospital floor, I'd have jumped right in. But before I could grovel again, he tapped his head. "I tell-a you what, boy. You help-a me in my shop, I teach-a you to fix-a things good. Is a deal?"

My jaw ached from the big fat smile I gave as I shook his hand. "Mr. C. – is a deal!"

8.
Treasure Trove

I was real excited by the time I reached home. Stumpy had asked to see some of my fixing-up, and I couldn't wait to show him. The juicer, I thought, and the tape deck, and the ....

I stood in the place where my stash should have been and groaned. Everything that was any good had disappeared. Everything! This time, I knew Stumpy hadn't taken it – so who was it? I was so furious I marched straight over to the Maxwells' to get Mungo. If he couldn't track the thief with that scabby nose of his, I'd use him as a guard dog and catch the *real* thief this time. I knocked on Mrs. Maxwell's door, but nobody was home. Still, they never took poor old Mungo out, so I walked around the side and called his name.

I heard a sort of muffled noise from his hole under the house. I bent down and peered into the gloom, careful not to meet him nose-to-dribbly-dog-nose. But dopey old Mungo didn't fill that hole. Skateboard, wall fan, birdcage, juicer ... all my treasures, stuffed in cardboard cartons, shoved down there like a pirate's secret cave! I was just about to climb inside when a shape moved in the shadows – a big human shape that lunged at me and snarled.

I think I must've broken an Olympic record, I jumped that fence so fast. By the time I reached Uncle Mo's office, I could hardly tell him what was up, and I was still puffing when the cops arrived. I watched through the fence as one of them squatted at the entrance to the hole and shone his flashlight inside. Suddenly he shouted something and disappeared into the hole. There were a lot of muffled thuds and cries – then everything was quiet again. A figure emerged from the hole, his hands cuffed behind him, pushed by the cop. Then I knew who my thief was – Crazy Ken, the jailbreaker! I guessed it must've been him who'd torched the limo too.

The cops took him away, snarling and cussing, and I carried home my precious stash. My face burned when I thought of how I'd accused Stumpy. That reminded me of the other deal I made with Stumpy at the hospital that day. "Time for me to lay-a the past to rest-a, boy," he'd said. "And-a for you too, I think-a."

I dug a hole in the corner of the yard, where the trees grow thick and no one ever goes. I buried Isabella's "silly old-a bones," tin and all, in a hole so deep that some little kid in China will probably dig it up some day. And when I'd hidden all signs of digging, I walked away. "Not that we forget-a," Stumpy's words echoed in my head, "but life, she is for living."

So that's my story. Y'know, it's funny I was always proud of being able to see the value in worn-out old things, but I almost missed the best find I ever made – Stumpy, or I should say, Edmondo. He and I are in business now, and he's a tough old teacher, but he sure knows his stuff.

There's just one more thing I can tell you, and you can make of it what you like. It's this: ever since I buried those two creepy little bones, it's like I can finally think about Mom without feeling all sick and strange.

Oh, yeah – and this. If I ever find another old bone, you can bet I'll bury it faster than you can say Edmondo Giovanni Alessandro Carducci.